Copyright @ 2021 Tehya Mae and Brett Lark, LLC

All rights reserved. No part of this book may be reproduced in any form or by any electronic or mechanical means, including information storage and retrieval systems, without permission in writing from the publisher.

ISBN Paperback: 978-1-953858-02-3

ISBN E-PUB: 978-1-953858-03-0

Library of Congress Control Number: 2021940357

Authors: Tehya Mae
Illustrator: Seriusrin
Editors: Brett Lark & Rebekah Vincent

Printed and bound in the United States of America
First printed February 2022

Published by Brett Lark, LLC
333 N 7th St #A
Burbank, CA 91501

One brisk autumn day, Jack and Cody were racing through the trees of a massive forest. Kids love to play here in this forest, and today Cody and Jack were pretending to be dragons, flying through the trees with speed and joy.

The two were having so much fun that they weren't paying attention. As Jack made a quick turn, he tripped over the roots of a large oak tree.

To both Cody and Jack's surprise, just beyond the tree was a sharp drop-off. And Jack was now careening through the air off the ledge!

The fall was not as hard as Jack feared, but was squishy and slimy instead. A large glob of shimmering pink slime waited below for Jack to land in. Cody scrambled down the hill to make sure his friend was all right and was surprised to see Jack covered in pink slime.

Now there are some things we just don't understand in this world, and one of them is that Jack, right where he stood, had transformed into a bonafide powerful dragon. Needless to say, Cody and Jack were taken aback with shock and astonishment at the transformation.

Have you ever dreamt of flying? Well, Cody and Jack are just like you, and once they discovered that Jack's new body came with a set of massive wings, Jack and Cody both thought the same crazy idea.

Cody and Jack flew over mountains and rivers, valleys and lakes. The two were having the greatest of times. They flew so fast that if you weren't paying attention, they would have sped right past your head without a trace, only a gust of wind hitting your neck.

Cody and Jack realized that they had a problem. How was Jack going to go back home? Would people do experiments on him or put him in a zoo? They both were hoping that Jack would just change back after a while. That wasn't the case so far. Jack thought that it might be lonely being the only dragon in the world, but their raspberry dinner kept them happy and spirited.

Well, wouldn't you know it, someone did see Jack flying that day. A greedy circus ringmaster had followed them to the farmhouse, and in the dead of night captured Jack, locking him in his circus truck. He was excited to make lots of money from all his fans as now his circus had the only dragon in the world!

Let me tell you, Jack was scared. For the ringmaster kept Jack caged in the center of the circus and showed him off three times a day to audiences from all over. The crowds were amazed and cheered with applause, but Jack had never felt more alone.

When all hope seemed lost, Jack was awakened by a familiar voice. It was Cody! He'd seen a poster of Jack for the circus and had come to break him out. Jack was so excited to see his friend that he had tears of joy streaming from his eyes.

Cody tried and tried to open the cage but was unable to crack it open. All of the sudden a burst of flames came from nowhere, hitting the lock and opening the cage. Cody and Jack were jolted with shock. Where did the flames come from?

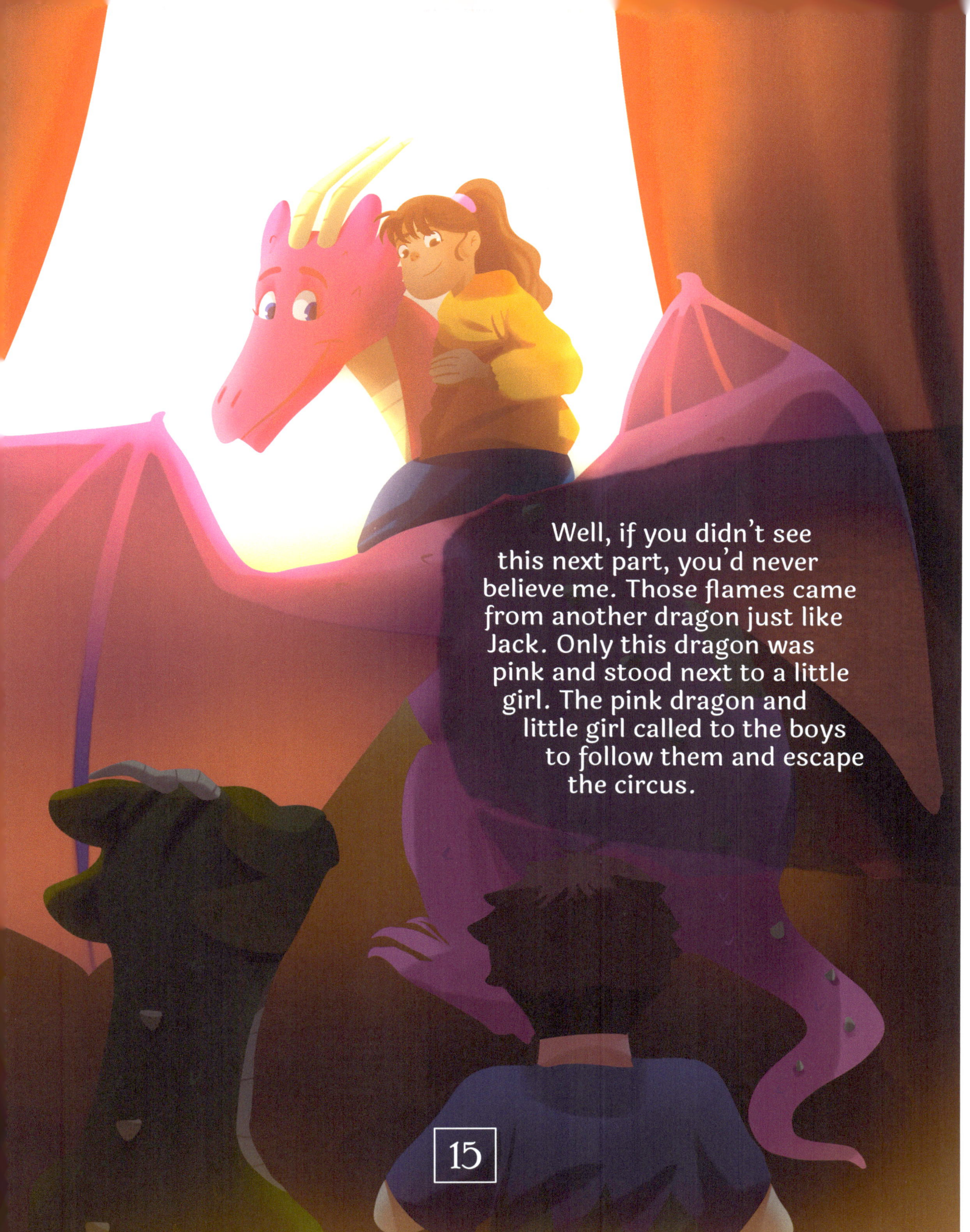

Well, if you didn't see this next part, you'd never believe me. Those flames came from another dragon just like Jack. Only this dragon was pink and stood next to a little girl. The pink dragon and little girl called to the boys to follow them and escape the circus.

The four were almost out
when the circus crew, led by their ringmaster,
threw a gigantic net over them. Now it wasn't just
Jack that was caught. The ringmaster would now have
two dragons for his circus! And he'd make sure their pesky
friends wouldn't cause any more problems ever again.

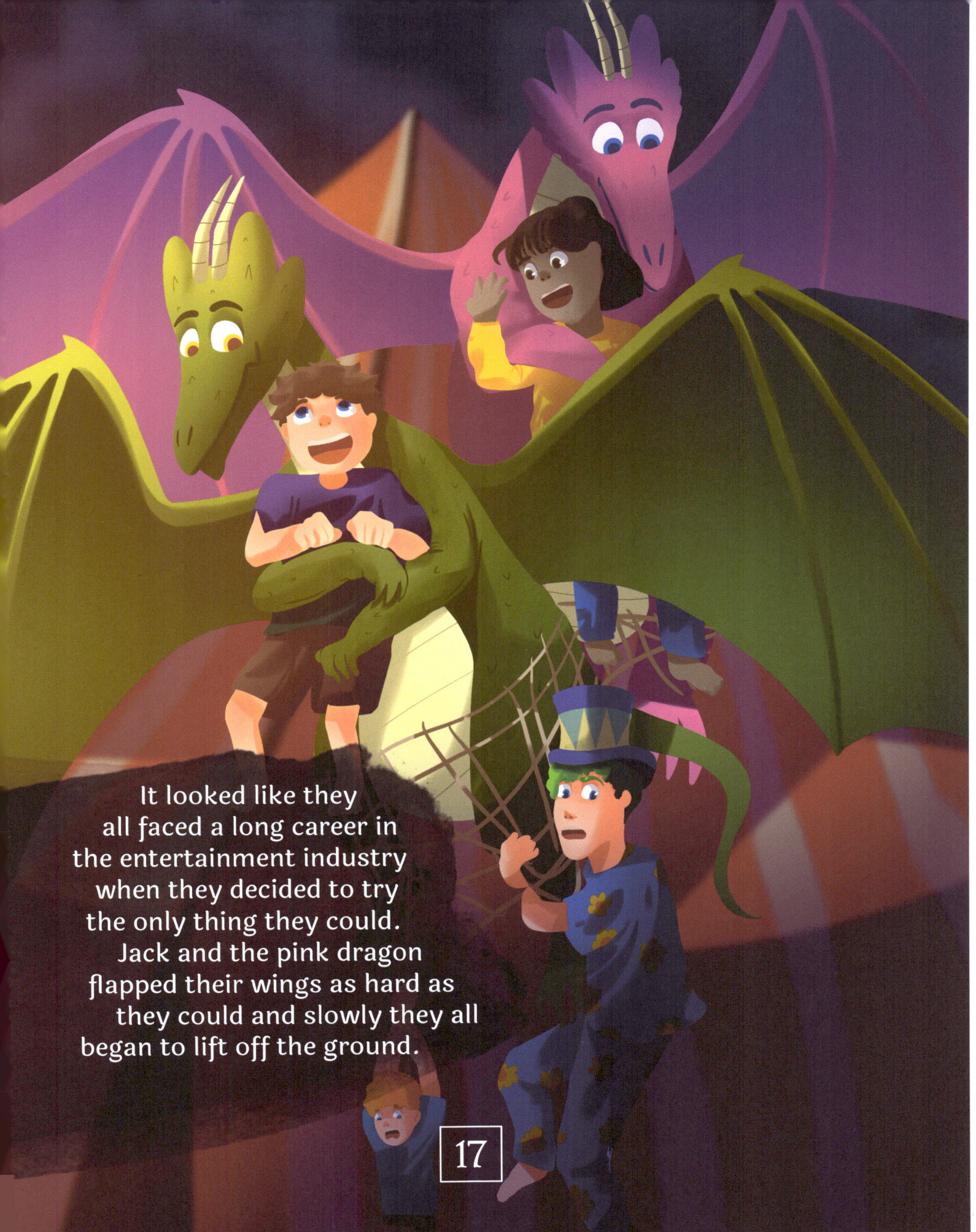

It looked like they all faced a long career in the entertainment industry when they decided to try the only thing they could. Jack and the pink dragon flapped their wings as hard as they could and slowly they all began to lift off the ground.

They flew higher and higher and soon all of them were far from the circus over a large lake. This was the moment! The kids and their dragon friends tossed off the net and all the crew and the ringmaster fell to a soft landing in the lake below.

Now away from danger, Jack and Cody introduced themselves and found out that the pink dragon's name was Jewel and her friend's name was Grace. But more amazing was that Jewel had once been a little girl who touched the pink slime in the forest. They decided that they needed to go back to the slime but for now enjoyed a beautiful sunrise.

They found the magical pink slime that had turned Jack and Jewel into dragons. All of them discussed what to do. Others could find the goo and be transformed into dragons. They had a responsibility to make sure that no one else got hurt.

So they made a decision.

CPSIA information can be obtained
at www.ICGtesting.com
Printed in the USA
BVHW021930300422
635816BV00002B/11